A CRY OUT OF TIME

By
J. L. Redington

©2012 J.L.Redington

No part of this publication may be reproduced, or stored in a retrieval system, or transmitted in any form or by any means, electronic, mechanical, photocopying, recording or otherwise, without written permission of the author.

PROLOGUE

The old Victorian house stood silently, a silence broken only by the gentle click, click of the gardening tools in the wrinkled hands of the caretaker, Ray. His wife, Louise, kneeling by his side, pulled steadily at the weeds starting up between the brilliantly colored flowers. The muffled roar of the great Pacific Ocean far below the cliff gave rhythm to their work while the musty sweet aroma of Salal, Oregon Blueberry and Pine filled the air.

Suddenly, from the attic window high above the front door came the shatter of breaking glass. Jumping to their feet, Ray and Louise ran back from the house to get a better look at the often repaired pane.

Floating in the window was the billowy form of their ghostly tenant. She gazed steadily at the aging couple. The intensity of her stare softened as she pleaded with the mortals standing below.

"Help me, please. Someone help me."

"Poor child," said Louise, shaking her head. "Poor, poor child."

Ray sighed and tapped the clippers in his hand. Then, as if unaware of the silhouette in the attic he announced cheerfully, "I think it's time for a vacation."

"Whatever gave you that idea?" Louise asked with surprise.

"Not what, my dear…who!" he said, waving his garden clippers toward the dejected form floating in the attic window.

***

## Chapter One

Esme blew her long dark hair back from her face as she bent to pick up her jeans from the bedroom floor. She hated cleaning her room. She hated putting her clothes away. Why didn't someone invent disposable clothes? Wear 'em once and throw 'em out. Now that was her kind of clothes! And if you should happen to drop them on the floor, they magically disappeared… just melting away. That was Esme's idea for the invention of the year.

She trudged to her dresser, pulled open the drawer with a sigh and shoved the somewhat folded jeans into a barely vacant spot in the mass of clothing. Pushing on the drawer with her backside, she surveyed the disaster that was her bedroom.

"One item down, one hundred fifty thousand to go," she whispered to no one in particular.

*That* was her life…whispering to no one in particular. Esme had a different name and everyone teased her about it. She was too thin, no matter how much food she consumed, and too tall compared to others her age. The kids at school made fun of her, except for a precious few she counted as her friends…two, to be exact. Esme had two friends, Vienne and Delaney, and she told them everything.

She was fifteen years old now, but when she was younger she'd begged her parents for a baby sister. She'd even have taken a baby brother if nothing else was available! But that never happened. Her parents had thought about adopting, but just never seemed to get around to it, and so there she was, tall, skinny Esme, with two friends, and a lot of time on her hands.

She walked to her mirrored dresser and plopped down on the small stool. She stared into the dark brown almond shaped eyes with their long lashes. Her shoulder length hair hung limply about her head, or so she thought. "What's wrong with a few natural curls and a little sheen?" she moaned.

From the intercom by the door on her wall came her mother's voice. "Dinner's on Es. Come on down. You can finish your room after you eat." Esme moaned a sarcastic "yippee" as she walked to the unit. Leaning back against the wall, she reached over her shoulder and pressed the reply button.

"K, Mom. I'll be right down." She opened her bedroom door and headed downstairs.

The kitchen and dining room were bustling with her mom and dad getting dinner on. Handing three plates stacked with three bowls to Esme, her dad smiled.

"Here beautiful. Make yourself useful."

She took the plates and bowls with a sigh and a smile and laid each plate in its place on the table with a bowl just below it. She loved that her dad thought she was beautiful, even though she knew he was just being her dad. She loved him for being her dad. Her mom was stirring something that smelled amazing and made Esme's stomach growl with anticipation. It was her famous homemade stew and rolls dinner. She hadn't even realized she was hungry until just this moment.

Her mom smiled as she entered the kitchen and said, "Would you put the silverware on, Es? Everything is just about ready."

Esme's parents were about as normal as you could ask for. Her mother stayed home mostly and worked on the computer. She wrote articles for magazines and had been published in several large publications, though Esme couldn't ever remember their names. Her mom was pretty busy with all the writing and then the prep for printing. She had deadlines, presentations, phone calls then more deadlines, more presentations and more phone calls. She liked her work and she always told people she was happy to be able to work from home so she could be there for Esme. People always said Esme got her face from her mother, but she didn't think they knew what they were talking about. She looked nothing like her mom! Her mom was petite, with an oval shaped face that made her brown eyes look huge. When she smiled her whole face smiled. She was thin, not skinny like Esme, just thin, perfectly thin. Her clothes always looked nice and she had a confidence that made Esme want to be like her. She loved her mom. She thought she was the most beautiful mom in the whole world.

She got everything else from her dad. He was a tall man, with long legs and long arms. He, too smiled easily, like her mom, and he made Esme and her mom laugh every day. Or at least it seemed like it was every day. He had sandy brown hair with a hint of curl(something she definitely did not inherit) and a wonderful dimple that was completely invisible until he laughed. Like Esme, his eyes were brown, too. She guessed that's why she didn't get the blue eyes she wished she'd gotten. Her dad worked at the hospital, not a doctor, but a Director of something or other. He made sure the departments at the hospital had the supplies they needed to run their part of the facility. He loved his job and worked hard at it, sometimes staying late into the evening.

They sat down to the dinner of thick homemade stew and rolls fresh from the oven. Her absolute favorite meal in the known universe! She ate with enthusiasm, and then realized no one was talking. She looked from her dad to her mom.

"What's up?" she asked around a mouthful of bread.

"Well," her dad said. "We wanted to talk to you about something, and since it involves your summer break, we thought we'd let you have some input. We've been invited to take our vacation on the Oregon Coast this summer."

Esme cocked her head, "Invited? How do you get 'invited' to go on vacation?"

"It would seem Uncle Ray and Aunt Louise would like to take a break from caretaking at the Heceta House. Do you remember hearing about the old Heceta House? It's by that cute little town…what was the name of it…?" her dad looked at her mom.

"Florence," said her mom, looking thoughtful. "I think it's called Florence."

"Yes, that's it," her dad said snapping his fingers. "You remember us talking about Florence and the Heceta House, right Es?"

Esme nodded. "Yeah, I remember. So they want us to come and house sit for them? Can't they just lock up and take a break?"

Her dad smiled, "No, not exactly. There are things that have to be taken care of daily. They can't just leave for a month. The yard needs mowing, the flower beds need weeding and there's a whole beach below the cliff that needs wading in," he winked at her mother.

"A BEACH!" Esme almost dropped her spoon. "I didn't even think about the beach! That would be so much fun! AWESOME! When do we leave?"

"Well, to tell you the truth, we didn't think

you'd want to go!" her mom said smiling. "We are going to have to do some work while we're there. We thought you'd want to stay and spend the summer with your friends here. I'm so glad you're up for this, because your dad and I really want to get away for a while. My work is slower this time of year and what work I have I can take with me. Dad has enough vacation time that we could stay for the month."

Esme couldn't help grinning. "I definitely want to go. Vienne and Delaney are both going to be gone and I wasn't really looking forward to the summer. I won't even have to clean my room. Everything I need is already out…I just have to put it in a suitcase. It's perfect!"

"Oh, no you don't," her mom said firmly. "You still have a room to clean, and those clothes go in the DIRTY clothes, not stuffed in your drawers."

Esme sighed. Bummer, she'd thought for a minute there she was free.

The family cleaned up the dishes as they talked about the places they would go see and the things they would be able to do. Esme was most excited about seeing the ocean. She'd never seen an ocean before and couldn't imagine water all the way to the horizon.

As she lay in bed that night, in her nicely cleaned room, Esme felt uneasy.

"What's my deal?" she said to herself. "It's

going to be a blast! Right? It's the coast, with an ocean and a beach. What could possibly be wrong with that?"

Still, as she closed her eyes and drifted off to sleep, she thought she could hear a child crying. It was a lonely cry, sad and afraid. As sleep took her, Esme dreamed she was reaching out toward the sound of the crying, and then it was gone.

## Chapter Two

The next month was a blur of finishing school, saying goodbye to Vienne and Delaney at least a dozen times and packing.  OH GOOD GRIEF!  Packing.  There was no end to it!  Should she take this, will she need that, how much *can* she bring?  The suitcase won't close.  Put some away, pull out some more.  It would take a month of trial and error just to get her 'needs' down to something that would fit into a suitcase the size of a walnut.  Nice.

She decided to take a break from the whole packing thing and called Vienne and Delaney, again, and they came over to say their goodbyes, again.  They sat on her bed side by side.

"So," said Vienne in her most matter of fact tone.  "I've done some looking into this place you're going to; this 'Heceta House'.  Vienne's shiny and perfectly straight blond hair was pulled back into a ponytail that bobbed excitedly as she spoke.  Her blue eyes sparkled and grew larger with each sentence.

"And by the way, it's not pronounced like it looks.  It's pronounced 'Huh-SEE-tuh' she said, with an obvious (and just a little obnoxious) accent on the "SEE".  "*And*", she announced proudly, "it's *haunted*!  Isn't that so cool?"  Esme and Delaney both gasped.

"I know!" squealed Vienne.  "It's just so awesome!  I wish we were going.  I want to see the ghost! I would talk to her, you know, and try to be her friend and--" She was interrupted mid sentence by Esme.

"*Her*? How do you know it's a 'her', and how to you know there's even a ghost there?" she asked, doubtfully.

"Well," announced Vienne with a smile, "because unlike *some* people I know, *I've* been on the Internet scoping out your vacation spot! It was just so much more interesting than going to visit cousins for a month like we're doing. It says there is a ghost there, and it's a little girl with the face of an old lady. How cool is that?"

Esme pulled out her laptop and plopped on her bed sitting with her legs folded in front of her. She rested the laptop on her legs and lifting the lid, turned it on and waited for it to boot. "So, you found this on the Internet? Why didn't I think of that?"

Vienne sat down on one side and Delaney followed on the other, all three sets of eyes glued to the monitor. Delaney was quite the opposite of Vienne, with chin length dark hair and a hint of curl and dark eyes that grew equally as large as Vienne's when she got excited. Clicking on the browser button, Esme did a Google search of "Heceta House Ghost, Florence Oregon.     "Look at that!" cried

Delaney. "It's all over the Internet about it being haunted!"

"Mmm hmm," Esme shook her head absently as she read aloud the notation on the screen.

"...*Though there have been no sightings at the lighthouse itself, the Heceta House is on the 10 most haunted houses in the United States.*" The girls ooooh'ed with spooky delight as Esme continued reading. *"Reports are numerous regarding the presence of the "Gray Lady", as referred to by those who have seen her. Some call her "Rue" in reference to an incident with a group using an Ouija Board. No one has found a record of a child being born at the Heceta House, but the headstone of an infant girl was found buried beneath the grass beside the house. There is a belief the Gray Lady is the mother of that child, unwilling to leave her infant. Others having seen the ghost believe it to be the child herself..."*

Esme's voice trailed off as the words sunk in.

"BUT," said Vienne dramatically, jumping suddenly from the bed and standing in front of the two girls, "Other things I've read say it's a child with an old woman's face! OH! I so want to see her!"

Her hands flew to either side of her face holding her head as if it was going to roll off her shoulders.

"That's easy for *you* to say, Vienne," moaned Esme, realizing the implications of actually seeing a ghost. "You're not the one that's *going* there!"

Vienne and Delaney said in unison, "But I wish I was!" The laughter that followed broke the serious spell in the room.

"What would you say to a ghost, anyway?" mused Esme, as the laughter quieted. She set the laptop aside and leaned her elbows on her folded legs. She lifted her head and gesturing with her hands continued, "I mean, do you casually walk up to her, wave your hand and say, "Hey there, Rue! My name is Esme! So, tell me, what's it like being a ghost?"

The girls said nothing, realizing for the first time there would be that awkward 'first sight' introduction.

Vienne sat back down on the bed. "Gosh," she said, "I hadn't thought of that. How would you even find her? Aren't ghosts invisible?"

"Well," said Delaney with a shrug of her shoulders, "if people have seen her, then she can't always be invisible, right? I mean, people *have* seen her!" She looked at the others expectantly.

"This gives me the creeps, you guys!" said Esme with a shiver. "I don't want to meet a ghost! I'm not even sure I even want to go now!"

"A little late for that," said Vienne. "You're leaving tomorrow, you know."

"Yeah, but, this is too weird!" said Esme. "I mean, if she's an old lady like the one article said, maybe she just wants to scare people. Think about it! If you were a ghost, what would your main motivation be? She walks around opening and closing cupboard doors and making noise! Why do you think she's doing that? Just for kicks?" she asked, "or to scare the *bajeebies* out of people? And if she wants to scare people, I'm not so sure I want to meet her."

"Well," said Delaney thoughtfully. "Maybe she's the little kid ghost and just wants someone to hang. I mean, you won't really know until you see her, and you're going to have to decide right now what your reaction is going to be when you do."

"That's a great idea," smiled Vienne, "just think about what you're going to say so you won't be afraid. Let's plan it out!"

"That's what I said before, you guys!" said Esme, exasperated. "Just exactly how do you start a conversation with a ghost?"

The room went silent once again as the girls thought through the dilemma of ghostly introductions. Sitting together on the bed all three were deep in thought, heads propped on fists, elbows on knees, staring intently at the floor.

Suddenly the bedroom door flew open as Esme's mother burst into the room with an armful of neatly folded laundry.

"Esme you really need to get packed. I've told you--"

She was stopped in her tracks as three girls screamed in unison and landed in a pile in the middle of the bed desperately clutching at each other.

"What in the world are you three doing?" she laughed in surprise. "Esme, you *really* need to get packed. Five more minutes with the girls and then it's time for them to go and you to get serious about packing."

The girls untangled themselves from the pile, smiling sheepishly.

"Okay, Mom," said Esme.

Her mother gave them that, "Silly girls" look. Then shaking her head and smiling she put the stack of clothes on the dresser, turned and walked from the room closing the door behind her.   Esme stared at her two confidantes and smiled sadly.

"I'm going to miss you guys," she said softly. "It would be so much more fun to have someone to sun bathe with on the beach." She turned back to the laptop, closed out of the internet and turned it off, shutting the lid with a familiar click.

"Yeah," said Delaney. "We're going to miss you, too. But you're going to have so much fun! I'm not even going to see cousins like you, Vienne. I'm going to be on a dumb cruise ship with nobody to do anything with. At least we'll both be at the ocean..." She smiled weakly.

"Yeah," said Esme, "I guess so. Then with an excited gasp Esme's face burst into a grin. "But here's what we should do! Let's all keep a diary of what we do each day so we can share it when we get back. That way, we'll remember what we did and not forget the good stuff."

"If there is any," whined Vienne.

"Oh there will be," smiled Esme excited for the first time. "Pact?"

"PACT!" cried the other two girls. Standing in a circle they placed right hands on right hands, pushed down and then lifted them into the air, wiggling their fingers and giggling with delight.

There was just something special about being BFF's.

## Chapter Three

It took some doing, but Esme actually did get packed with the help of her mother, and she did get her room picked up with no help from anyone. She'd made quite a mess trying to figure out what to take. It was seven a.m. when the alarm went off beside her bed.

She yawned and stretched and then remembered that today was the day they were flying to Oregon! "All RIGHT!" she yelled as she moved the covers and sat on the side of her bed. She'd only been on an airplane one other time in her whole life and she was too little to remember it, so today felt like her first time ever flying.

She dressed quickly, folding her PJ's and placing them under her pillow. She had others in her suitcase, so she didn't need to worry about trying to fit these in. She slipped into her blue jeans and favorite pink t-shirt. After putting on her shoes and socks she headed downstairs with her suitcase and carryon bag. Her carryon bag completed her "travel ensemble", and contained her computer and charger, pencil, paper, a book to read, iPod, and a few extra

CD's in case she got tired of the hundreds of songs she already had on it. She'd charged her computer the night before so she would have enough battery for the flight from her home in St. Joseph, Missouri to the Portland airport in Oregon.

Her dad was at the bottom of the stairs. "Hey gorgeous! Are you ready for this?"

Esme smiled and handed over the baggage. "I was born ready. What time does our flight leave, again?"

Her dad smiled and said, "Nine a.m., so we'll need to be ready to hop in the Cab when it gets here. We'll eat breakfast at the airport once we're through the check in."

"Cool," grinned Esme. She loved eating out!

After the ride to the airport, they found a nice restaurant and enjoyed a great breakfast of whatever they wanted. Esme got one of those huge cinnamon rolls and some hot chocolate to dip it in. It was delicious, and she savoured every bite. Between mouthfuls she talked excitedly about the Oregon Coast Aquarium, the Wax Museum and Sea Lions in Old Town Newport, just up the coast from the Heceta House. Oh and not to forget the Sea Lion Caves close by. There would be so much to see! So many places to go!

"Yes, but don't forget," said her dad between bites of pancakes. "We do have work to do while we're there. We'll need to make sure we get the weeding done and prepare the house for the guests and visitors that will come when Uncle Ray and Aunt Louise get back. It doesn't all have to be done at once, but we do have to get it done."

"I know," said Esme. "It's just so exciting. I can't wait to get there!"

They headed down the wide walkways, past several gates with boarding passengers and finally stopped at the gate where their plane sat, ready for takeoff. As they entered the ramp to board, Esme's excitement level rose dramatically. She was actually going to fly in a plane! They found their seats by the numbers on the overhead baggage compartments. The pleading look in Esme's eyes made her parents smile and both agree to let her sit in the window seat.

Her favorite part of the whole flying experience was the takeoff. As the plane taxied down the runway, the landscape outside her window sped by faster and faster and faster. She could feel herself being pressed into her seat as the nose of the plane lifted. There was a moment of what felt like weightlessness as the wheels left the runway and the plane rose slowly into the sky. The engines roared and carried them swiftly upward. The cars on the road below looked like toys and the houses like pieces from a Monopoly game. How different the world looked from way up here.

As the seatbelt light switched off, Esme reached for her carryon bag and pulled out her diary. She stared at the page for a minute and realized she didn't want to write, so she put the diary back in the bag and pulled out her book.

"*No*," she thought to herself, "*I don't want to do that either*."

She couldn't take her eyes from the window as much as she tried, and she was so thankful her parents had let her take the window seat. She saw mountains now miniaturized by the distance between the plane and the land below. Small lines she knew were rivers wove their way through tiny little canyons as wisps of clouds floated just below the plane. It was mesmerizing to watch and she just couldn't bring herself to do anything but look out the window.

She thought about Vienne and Delaney and wondered what they were doing and when they were leaving on their vacations. As she gazed out the window, her eyelids became heavy and she leaned back in her seat, fighting to keep her eyes open. The clouds floating slowly below only added to the tired weight of her now drooping eyelids. She felt so sleepy, and so, so...

Short. She felt short, definitely shorter than she was used to feeling. The large wooden ship pitched up and down in the middle of an angry ocean. The vessel was very long, and sat low in the water, causing waves to crash over the side with each downward motion of its bow. The deck was slick with sea water and the girl held tight to anything she could get her hands on! The beautiful necklace her grandmother had given her before the voyage hung from her neck. She could still hear her grandmothers voice, "Keep this safe my love, and it will do the same for you. It's very special to me, but I want you to have it." So, loving and trusting her grandmother like she always had, and still struggling to hang onto the post she was standing by, she took the necklace and tucked it safely inside the neckline of her dress. It was cold against her skin, but it was safe. Just then the ship lurched forward and she wrapped her arms tighter around the post to keep from falling.

There were many passengers, but she couldn't make out any of their faces. It was like she was looking through a tunnel with only the center clear, everything else was blurred. The sky was dark and rain poured from the thick, black clouds. The ships engine roared and she could smell oil as it rose and fell in the wild seas. Salt water sprayed her face again, dampening her clothing. She looked around searching for something...for someone.

*"No, something and someone,"* she thought, holding desperately to the post.

Terror rising, she searched passengers and ship, looking and looking! The girl staggered along the deck, holding tightly to the railing now, trying to keep her balance as the ship pitched back and forth and up and down. People hurrying by her called out to loved ones in muffled voices that echoed in her head. She moved along the deck sliding and reaching for posts or railings as she made her way through the throng of terrified people, fear bubbling in her throat.

*"Where are they?"* she cried to herself, trying to be brave. "*Where are they?*"

The clouds overhead were the blackest she'd ever seen, the rain falling so hard it stung her face as it poured from the sky. Still she was looking, searching as panic welled inside her. She called out to them, but couldn't hear her own voice, couldn't understand who it was she was calling for.

*"Where are you?"*

The more she tried to see the more fear engulfed her as she gripped the deck railings.

Suddenly she was swooped into two strong arms that wrapped around her and hugged her tight. It was him! It was who she was looking for! She threw her arms around his neck, looking into the face of the father she loved so much.

*"Papa!"* she cried out, burying her face in his large shoulder. His kind face was full of concern, but in his arms she was safe. His dark hair was wet from the rain and water dripped from his head and face. She didn't care, she'd found him!

"We must find Mother, little one. Don't be afraid. We'll be ok."

He was breathing heavily and moving quickly through the people, weaving and turning, trying to hold on as the ship rolled violently through each wave.

*"Yes! That was it!"* she thought as she hugged him tighter, *"Mama! We have to find Mama."*

And then suddenly she was there, Mama was there, holding onto she and Papa. The frenzied noises of the people grew louder and more terrified. The three travellers found a place away from the ships railings and huddled together against a wall with an overhang offering precious little protection from the rain. She looked at the woman, so beautiful. Sea and rain water soaked the blonde hair in a bun on the back of her head. She wore no makeup, but didn't seem to need it. Her dark eyes were wide with concern, her face wet from the spray of waves and the downpour of rain. She looked at her husband. There were questions in her eyes, but she didn't speak. The noise from the boat and the passengers was deafening now, and it echoed through the air and rain.

The child looked through the crowd, still searching as her eyes finally found the last of those she searched for. The lumbering shape of the sandy colored Great Dane was weaving through the people, coming right toward her. As usual, he appeared to be smiling at her, somehow unaffected by the turmoil surrounding him. He was the biggest dog she'd ever seen. His head came almost to her shoulders when she'd stood by him as they'd played on the deck earlier that day and throughout the voyage. Seeing him through the crowd she jumped from her father's arms and ran to the dog. Wrapping her arms around his massive neck she felt his warm tongue licking her face.

"LaRue! Come back!" she heard vaguely behind her. But she couldn't leave her beloved friend. She had to make sure he was okay.

"Butler! Where have you been?" she cried, hugging him tightly. "I've been looking all over for you! Are you okay?" The warm tongue confirmed he was indeed okay and she hugged him again. "I love you, Butler. You're my best friend!"

Her parents were trying desperately to get to her through the crowd of now frantic people. They called loudly for her to come back, but the deck was getting more and more crowded. As she clung to Butler, she turned and reached toward her parents.

Suddenly there was a loud crack as lightening struck the mast. The ship lurched violently and the child screamed as her mama and papa reached for her, but it was too late. The decking broke away between them and people screamed as they flew into the sea, the back of the ship falling slowly away from the front. Instantly she and Butler were thrown in the opposite direction of her parents, as she screamed, "Mama! Papa!"

She hit the water, sinking beneath the waves, kicking her feet so hard her shoes came off. The dress she wore became heavy with water and pulled at her as she tried to make her way to the surface. Salty sea water filled her lungs and stomach and she coughed, sucking in more cold water. She felt something come up under her and gently nudge her upward. It was Butler! She grabbed his large neck and let him pull her up. As her face broke the surface, she coughed and choked, trying to breath. She looked up in time to see a big piece of the ship falling toward her. She screamed one last time and everything went black...

Esme jerked forward, sitting straight up and mumbling softly and breathlessly, "We have to help her!"

She looked around and realized she was in the airplane, her parents beside her.

Her mother looked at her in surprise. "You were dreaming Es, you're alright."

She spoke softly, reassuringly. She gave her a quick squeeze and went back to her book.

"It was so real! I was in a shipwreck and I was drowning!"

Esme's chest heaved up and down as though she were completely out of breath.

"There was a dog there, and he was helping me. It was so real!"

Her lungs felt like they would never have enough air in them again as she struggled to breathe. Her parents looked at her with an empathy born of soothing away many bad dreams.

"What!" she demanded. "It was really scary,Mom, it was real!" She looked from her mom to her dad.

Settling comfortably back in his seat, her dad said, "Well, it was just a dream, Es. You're fine. Take some deep breaths and shake it off."

Her mom patted her shoulder and returned to her book and Esme stared out the window once again. But she was far from forgetting the experience. She took a deep breath and looked out the window. She missed Butler.

"*I miss BUTLER?*" she thought incredulously. *"How can I miss a dog I've never even met?!"*

## Chapter Four

The plane ride proceeded uneventfully, with the exception of Esme reviewing the dream in her mind over and over again. She recorded the event in her journal so she could share it with Vienne & Delaney when she got home. She was still feeling very unsettled about the dream, but decided she would do as her dad suggested and shake it off. She spent the rest of the flight listening to music on her iPod and watching out the window.

Soon the family was walking through the Portland airport on their way to baggage claim. They picked up their bags after a short wait and headed to the car rental lot. Once they got the keys to the car and were shown where it was parked, they loaded up their baggage and before long were headed down the freeway toward Florence.

It was a beautiful drive and the lush green of the countryside mesmerized everyone as they travelled the freeway heading south. Green fields lay on either side of the road with tree covered hills. After a brief discussion about where to stop for a walk and stretch, they stopped at a rest stop nestled among tall pine trees and stretched their legs.

"It smells different here," said Esme.

"You're right, Es," her dad said. "They get a lot of rain in the winter and spring months, which makes for wet ground and beautiful trees and bushes. It's amazing how green it is here, even in the winter."

After a few minutes they piled back in the car and began again heading south to Florence. There was much to see and much to talk about. Esme especially liked the Coast Range with the sections of logged mountainside.

"It looks like a giant shaved those hills with his electric razor," She said laughing. They travelled west, through the lush green forests and finally came to the Siuslaw River that would guide them into Florence.

"What a funny name for a river," smiled Esme.

"Well," her dad said, "from what I've read this river is named after an Indian Tribe who used to live in this part of the coast."

"Were there a lot of Indians in Oregon?" asked Esme.

"There were many different tribes throughout the West, Es," he replied.

They turned at Mapleton and headed due west along the River. Fishing boats dotted the river with houses along the shore, some small, some large and rambling. It seemed peaceful and serene.

"What a beautiful place, "said her mother. "It just feels so stress free here."

"Well," said her dad, "that's because work is about fifteen hundred miles away."

They laughed, glad for the time away. Esme was glad as well. Her parents were much more fun when they didn't have to work all the time. She guessed everyone was probably more fun when they didn't have to work.

Soon they rounded a corner and drove straight into the quaint coastal town of Florence. Highway 101 ran right through the middle of the town from north to south. There were stores, motels, restaurants and gas stations lining either side of the highway. The smell of the ocean was everywhere. Esme rolled down her window to get a better view, and to smell the wonderful crisp, fresh coastal air. She couldn't help but smile as the wind tossed her long dark hair across her face.

Everyone was hungry since leaving the airport, so they stopped at a local pizza restaurant not far from the turnoff that would take them north to the Heceta House and Lighthouse.

"This is the best pizza I've ever had," exclaimed Esme with a mouthful. "Let's come back and have it again while we're here." That was a definite agreement from all parties and they ate with enthusiasm, enjoying every bite.

When no one could hold another ounce of pizza they asked for a box to take the remaining pieces with them. They took their box of leftovers and headed to the car. Soon they were on the road once more, driving north to Devils Elbow.

Heading up Highway 101 they came to the first of many spots where there was a clear view of the ocean.

"Oh, Dad! Pull off! Pull off! Can we stop and see it?" said Esme enthusiastically.

"Sure," smiled her father, driving the car onto the gravel pullout.

Jumping out of the car, Esme ran to the railing at the edge of the bluff. The sun was approaching the horizon and the smooth water sparkled like a million diamonds. The soft rumble of waves rolling over the sand floated up from the beach below. There were people on horseback riding slowly in single file along the shoreline.

"Can we do that, Mom? Can we, Dad?" Esme pointed.

"That would be a fun thing to do," said her mother. "We'll have to plan an evening to come and do the sunset ride. What a great idea."

Esme stared out over the vast expanse of water. She'd never seen so much water in one place. The memories of her dream earlier on the plane nudged her and suddenly she felt like she already knew how cold that water was, and how threatening it could be.

*"I think deep sea fishing is definitely off my to-do list,"* she thought to herself.

She slowly backed away from the railing, remembering the fall through the air and into the sea. She could still feel the water pulling at her shoes and clothes, the relief of Butler as she wrapped her arms around him and let him guide her to the surface. She could still see that huge ship coming right at her.....

"Esme! Esme, are you ok?" Her mother was gently shaking her. "Honey? What's the matter? Es?"

"Oh, sorry," she said coming back to the present. "I was just remembering that dream on the plane. It was so real!" Her dad was standing beside her and heaved a sigh of relief when he heard her words.

"Let's get going," he said eyeing Esme, "we should be close now, and I think Uncle Ray and Aunt Louise will want to head out as soon as we get there."

They drove for a few more minutes North on Highway 101 and soon came to Devils Elbow State Park. They crossed the beautiful old bridge and shortly after, turned off the highway into the overgrown driveway leading to the Heceta House. As they rounded a curve in the drive, the amazing old home came into view. Just like the pictures, it was an old Victorian style home with a red roof and white washed siding. There was a white picket fence surrounding the property and deep green undergrowth with amazing tall pines nestled in the area all around the cliff.

Exiting the car, Esme's senses were assaulted by what felt like a hundred different colors and smells. It was so green it actually *smelled* green. Well, if green had a smell, Esme thought it would smell like this. The fragrant underbrush and trees blended with the scent of the ocean far below the cliff. The mixture was invigorating, refreshing and *marvellous.*

She took a deep breath, and gazed around her with eyes not quite wide enough to take it all in. As she stopped turning, she found herself facing the beautiful old house, a stark white and red against the green undergrowth and blue sky. She stared at the house, gazing at each board, each window and the beautiful covered porch with its white railing and white columns. It was everything she thought it would be, and more.

Her thoughts were interrupted by an eruption of voices from the porch as Uncle Ray and Aunt Louise came out the door and down the walk to meet their guests. Uncle Ray was tall and thin with tufts of wild dark hair that wiggled and waved in the ocean breezes. His warm and friendly eyes blended well with the soft wrinkles of his face, and instantly Esme knew she would like him. Aunt Louise was quite the opposite, when it came to build. She was round, everywhere, with gray hair that sat at the back of her head in a perfect bun. Like Uncle Ray, her face was warm and friendly and made you feel welcome instantly.

There was a lot of hugging and laughing and grinning as they walked up to the porch. Dad wasn't kidding when he said they would be ready to leave once her family got there. Their bags were at the door waiting for loading. Once they had shown the family around the house, explained the list of daily and weekly chores and answered any questions the family had, Ray and Louise grabbed their bags and were out the door, heading down the drive toward Highway 101.

Standing on the walk in front of the house, Esme looked up at the window pane on the front of the house. Was there really a ghost there? Was she really a busy ghost, opening and closing cupboards and switching on lights for no reason? What made her do these things, and was she an old lady or a little girl?

Esme had so many questions, and wondered if she'd ever get to meet this spirit resident. Which made her wonder all over again what she'd do if she ever really did meet her. She looked around at the last of the light fading with the setting sun.

*"What an amazing place,"* she thought to herself. *"What a--"* Her thoughts were interrupted by a loud and piercing scream coming from the house. Without thinking Esme ran into the house yelling for her mother.

"Mom! Mom! Where are you? What's wrong?" She cried frantically searching the living room. Her mother came out of the kitchen casually wiping her hands on a dish towel as she stared at her daughter.

"Esme, whatever are you yelling about?" She asked with a smile, then continuing on she said, "Isn't this the most gorgeous old house? I haven't seen architecture like this since I was a kid. And just look at this fireplace! Isn't it amazing?"

"Mom!" said Esme, exasperated, "Didn't you hear that scream? How could you not hear it? Where's Dad? Is he okay?"

"Oh good grief, Es," said her Mom. "Dad is right here in the kitchen with me. There wasn't any scream. Don't get started on that silliness you and your friends were talking about. You're just going to freak yourself out if you do. Come on let's eat the rest of that pizza."

"But Mom..."

"I mean it, Esme," she warned. "It'll be a very long four weeks if you're going to keep this up."

Her mother walked casually back into the kitchen smiling again at the architecture and style of the old house. Esme glanced around the living room and with a quick squeal, darted after her mother and into the kitchen.

## Chapter Five

The next day dawned sunny, breezy and gorgeous. Esme bounded out of bed and down the stairs to see what smelled so good. She walked into the kitchen as her Mom and Dad were reviewing the "to do" list left by Uncle Ray and Aunt Louise.

"So," said her Dad. "There's weeding and mowing to do today. What's your pleasure?" He looked at his daughter expectantly.

"Me? Today?" she gasped. "Can't we have just one day to play before we get into the work stuff? I really wanted to walk up to the lighthouse and explore the woods and the beach. I mean, sheesh! The BEACH, Dad. The BEACH!"

Her parents laughed and her Mom said, "We're just teasing you, Es. We would love to walk up to the lighthouse and check it out...and we were thinking it would be a perfect day for a picnic on the beach. We thought we'd pack up some lunch and take it down for a picnic. What do you think?"

"Awesome!" smiled Esme. "What's for breakfast? It smells so good."

"Oh," said her Mom, "just some old bacon and moldy eggs." Esme smiled as she sat down at the table.

"Sounds like my favorite breakfast," she smiled, picking up her knife and fork.

"Do you think we can go to Newport and see the Aquarium sometime?" asked Esme between bites. "And I want to see the dunes, too, in Florence. And Vienne said you could feed Sea Gulls at Yachats, and--"

"Whoa there, Gorgeous," laughed her Dad. "We do have to spend *some* time working, you know."

"Yeah, I know, but how often are we going to get to come to Oregon? I wanna see stuff while we're here, you know?" said Esme eagerly, with a little drama added for good measure.

"Yes, we know," said her Mom picking up the plates. "We'll see as much as we can, but we do have to pay for our room and board here." She winked as she turned to the sink. "Now help me clear the table so we can get up to that lighthouse." Working together they cleared away the breakfast dishes and wiped the table. Esme couldn't wait to get outside and see what was there.

Before long, they were walking up the paved pathway leading to the old lighthouse, laughing and teasing each other. The now familiar smell of the undergrowth and trees filled the air. As they crested the hill, the huge light came into view. It stood tall and white against the deep blue sky, its red roof a stark contrast to the whitewashed sides.

"Wow," whispered Esme looking up at the tall building." It's sure a lot bigger in real life." She craned her neck to see all the way to the top.

"Yes, it's very impressive," said her Dad. "And would you look at that ocean," he said turning. "It's just beautiful." They walked around the base of the lighthouse, checking out the rocks, the trees and smelling the amazing coastal air.

There was a wood fence bordering the edge the cliff with a paved walkway beside it. Grass filled in the area between the walkway and the lighthouse. There were rocks at the base of the light and behind them were more trees and brush. The air was crisp and the sky a most beautiful blue. The ocean murmured softly far below.

Esme walked to the railing. She held her hand over her eyes and looked out at the vast expanse of ocean. Her eyes stopped scanning as she squinted to make out a shape moving quickly through the water. She pulled on her father's sleeve and pointed to a ship that looked like it was coming right at the shore.

"Look, Dad. That's weird, isn't it, a ship coming right at us?" her dad looked out over the ocean.

"I don't see it, Es. Where are you looking?"

"It's right there, Dad." she said, pointing straight out from the cliff. "Ships shouldn't be able to go that fast, should they? It's coming awfully fast for being that close to a shore, don't you think?" She said continuing to point at it.

"Just look at that thing go!" She was still shielding her eyes from the sun as she continued to stare at the fast approaching ship. In the short amount of time since she'd first seen it, the ship had almost reached the cliff.

"Oh my gosh!" she cried in alarm, "it's going to hit the cliff, Dad! It's coming too fast! It won't be able to turn in time!"

She pointed frantically in the direction of the ship. Her parents were anxiously searching the ocean, unable to find a ship anywhere.

"How can you *not* see that?" she shouted in frustration, "look at it! It's going to hit! It's going to hit! We have to do something!"

Her Dad grabbed her shoulders and spun her around to face him. "Esme! Stop it!" There is no ship--"

But by this time Esme was screaming hysterically as she forced herself from her father's grip and leaned over the railing, watching the ill fated ship as it ran into the cliff... and disappeared.

*And disappeared?* She stared at the cliff in disbelief.

"It...it was right there, Dad. It was. Mom? It was there, didn't you see it?" Her voice was trembling and she could barely choke out the words.

"Honey," said her Mom. "Maybe it was a bird. There was no ship. Dad and I wouldn't kid about something like that. You can see there is nothing there, Es, nothing." Her Mom gave her a squeeze and looked into her eyes, brushing a lock of hair back from her face.

"I...I don't understand. It was a ship, coming right for the cliff," she said weakly, "I saw it. I did see it. I did."

"Okay, Es. You saw what you saw. I don't understand it either, but let's just head back to the house. Maybe a good stiff soda will calm your nerves." Her dad smiled at her reassuringly and gave her a squeeze.

Esme wiped her nose with on the sleeve of her hoodie. "Okay... Yeah. It's okay... I'm...I'm...fine. I...maybe I...yeah. Okay, let's just go."

They walked quietly back down the path to the house. She could see her parents looking at each other in worried disbelief. She knew what they were thinking. It really wasn't like Esme to get hysterical over something. She just wasn't the hysterical type, and she knew that's what worried her parents the most. They continued walking in silence. Esme could hear voices, soft and garbled. Someone was whispering words she couldn't understand, words she couldn't quite hear. Eventually Esme turned to her mom.

"What?" she asked looking at her.

"I didn't say anything," said her mom, a little more relaxed. "I'm just thinking about this place and how amazing it is."

Her Mom smiled at her. She gave her another squeeze.

"Are you feeling better?"

Esme looked at her mother.

"You didn't just say something to me?" asked Esme again.

"Nope, not me," said her mom.

They continued on and the whispers returned. She was beginning to get irritated.

Turning to her parents she said emphatically, "I can't hear you, what did you say?"

Her parents both stopped and looked at her with blank stares. Esme walked a couple of steps and stopped, too, looking at her parents.

"What?" she said, exasperated, "it just sounds like you're whispering or mumbling. What did you say?" She looked at each of them.

"Honey, I think we need to get your ears checked," joked her Dad. "You're hearing things."

Her Mom put her arm around her shoulder and they started walking again.

Esme looked at her parents.

"But I heard--" she stopped, changing her mind. "No, it was nothing. Never mind, it must have been the wind."

But in her heart she knew it wasn't the wind. She'd heard voices, whispers, lots of them. She'd seen a ship disappear right into the cliff. She wondered if this whole ghost thing was getting to her. Maybe she was just thinking about it too much. But that was just it...she hadn't even been thinking about the ghost at all this morning. Was she going crazy? She didn't know but she did know one thing; her parents weren't going to hear any of the things she was hearing or see any of the things she was seeing.

*"Where are you Delaney and Vienne when I need you the most!"* she thought anxiously to herself.

After packing the picnic lunch and changing into swim suits the family gathered some towels, a couple folding beach chairs and a blanket and headed to the beach. They walked down the path leading from the cliff. Esme looked back up at the house as they made their way to the beach.

*"Man!"* she thought, *"if there* is *a ghost in that house, she sure is making herself scarce."*

## Chapter Six

The beach was incredible! Esme was entranced by the waves washing up on the shore and how the water left behind would lazily lap at her feet before it followed the tide back out. It was soon replaced by another and then another and yet *another* wave. It seemed so endless and so relaxing. The soft murmur of the waves and the warm sun on her back almost made her sleepy as she dipped her feet into the water, almost made her forget the experience at the lighthouse. Almost. The wet sand held the imprints of her feet until the new waves softly rolled in and washed them away. It was mesmerizing.

No one else was on the beach just yet, as it wasn't even eleven in the morning. It had been an interesting day already.

Sitting just at the edge of the waters reach, her knees to her chest, Esme watched the water roll in around her. She heard someone call her name, and turned to her parents to see what they wanted. They sat in their beach chairs, completely immersed in their reading.

*"Esme…"*

She jumped to her feet and looked wildly around the beach, but saw nothing. Her parents hadn't moved.

*"I'm here, Esme. We're here, and we've been waiting for you to come to us for a very long time."*

"Who are you? *Where* are you?" Esme asked, bewildered. She continued searching the beach for the source of the voice she was hearing.

*"Think your words…think, don't speak…"* as the words floated through her head, she realized she wasn't hearing the words with her ears, she was hearing them in her *head.*

*"How can that be? How can I hear you, but not with my ears? How are you doing that?"*

There was a ripple in the air to her right, and Esme turned just as the graceful form of a very big dog walked through what appeared to be an invisible wall. The familiar form of the Great Dane lumbered gracefully toward her.

*"I am here, I have always been here waiting… for you. We've both been waiting for you."*

Esme stood stunned as she stared down the beach at the magnificent animal walking slowly toward her.

*"Butler,"* she whispered. Then thinking to herself she said, *"But, how can this be? I saw you in my dream…you're just a dream. How can you be here?"*

*"Because I am not flesh, young Esme,"* said the voice floating through her head. Butler padded over to her and sat down on his haunches beside her, facing the ocean.

Esme stared at him amazed again at how huge he was, amazed he was sitting there, so…*there*. His head came to her upper arms, his ears a little higher than that. In the dream she remembered he was as tall as her shoulder, but she also remembered feeling shorter. She didn't know what to say, or what to think. Her mind was crammed with questions she didn't know how to ask. She stared at this dog she truly did feel love for, a dog from a dream she was beginning to feel wasn't a dream at all.

*"That's right, Esme. It wasn't a dream at all."*

He was looking at her now, searching her face. His eyes were warm and kind and Esme felt his wisdom as she looked back at him.

*"I think this is going to take some getting used to,"* she thought, staring at Butler. She jumped as he chuckled at her words.

*"I think we're going to get along just fine. We have always been friends, you and I. Since that ship you were never on, sank into this ocean you'd never seen before, ending a precious life you only briefly experienced."*

With those words, his eyes seemed to smile at her. He stood on four huge feet, looked into her face, then turning, lumbered slowly away from her down the beach, disappearing into a wall that wasn't there.

"What do you see, Es?" called her mom.

Esme was jolted out of her thoughts and back to a vacant beach. She didn't know how long she'd stood there staring at nothing. Literally…nothing. She turned to her parents and forced a smile.

"Oh, nothing," she said. "It was nothing."

Boy, was that a mouthful. She'd just seen a dog that was in her dream that wasn't a dream. He said they had been waiting for her. They? Who is they, and how did they know she was coming? What had he meant by that?

"He knew about my dream," she said aloud as she turned back to the vast ocean. She sat back down, with her knees pulled up to her chest again.

"He remembered me from *my* dream." She tried to make sense of it, tried to put pieces together, but it was like they all belonged to the wrong puzzle.

She'd felt no fear, only the same warm friendship she'd felt for him on the ship. He was so familiar to her, like she had known him for a very long time. She knew him to be gentle and kind. She knew he would never hurt her, indeed, she knew he would protect her. She knew these things and couldn't help but wonder if she was losing her mind.

*"No, my friend, you're not losing your mind."* There was that soft chuckle again. *"You'll understand in time. Just don't take too much time. That is a thing we don't have a lot of."*

She looked around again, but there was no one there. This time, however, she knew who was talking to her. She wanted to see Butler, again. Actually, she couldn't wait to see him again.

## Chapter Seven

It was late in the afternoon when the family began gathering their things to return to Heceta House. At least her parents had been able to relax, but Esme felt like she was wound tighter than an eight day clock. She didn't know exactly what that meant, it was her grandmother's saying, but it had a lot to do with feeling stressed. And she felt stressed!

"Why so quiet, Es?" her father's voice floated on the breeze somewhere outside her head.

"Hmm?" she responded, half listening.

"It's not like you to be so quiet. You're usually lining up our next day's activities for us," he smiled.

"Oh, I was just thinking about how beautiful the ocean is, and how amazing it must be to live here year around," which wasn't actually what she was thinking about at all.

"Well," smiled her mother, "then it sounds like if we want any peace and quiet at our house, we'd better move to the coast."

"Yeah, I guess," said Esme, trying to be light. But somehow, she couldn't get Butler out of her head. He was there, permanently. She felt like she could almost hear him breathing, almost feel him beside her, yet he wasn't there, and she was pretty sure she couldn't be hearing him breathe. It wasn't actually a physical thing, a thing you could touch or see or feel. It was a…a…oh geez. There was no way to say it without sounding completely mental….but it was…well…mental, like she could *'feel'* him in her mind.

She could vaguely hear her parents discussing the chores list and talking together, but their conversation seemed distant. She couldn't help wondering…what in the world was she thinking? Had she lost her mind? No, Butler said she hadn't. But would an animal you conjured up in a dream be honest with you? Oh good grief. She could walk this emotional circle for a century and never figure it out…at least that's what it felt like.

They arrived back at the house and Esme went to her room to change. She put her dirty clothes on the floor and dressed in clean jeans and a t-shirt. Turning to pick up the clothes, she saw they were on her bed.

"Either I need to pay better attention, or I'm losing my mind," she said to herself. She turned around again, and saw the drawer she'd just shut, hanging open.

"Okay, Esme, now you're *really losing it.*"

She shut the drawer, picked up the dirty clothes from off the floor and started for the door. From off the *floor*?

"Didn't I just put those on the…?"

She turned slowly and looked at the bed.

"Nah," she said, shaking her head. "Now I'm just imagining things."

She put the clothes in the hamper and headed down the stairs. She could hear her mother in the kitchen starting dinner.

"Gee, Mom," she said as she entered the kitchen door. "Kind of early for--" She stopped as she saw a girl curiously opening and closing cupboards, inspecting the counter and checking the table. The ghost turned as Esme entered, looking directly at her. She smiled, waved to Esme, and giggling a playful giggle, ran into the wall. Not like Esme would run into a wall, but ran into the wall and just kept going *into* the wall.

"Mom? Dad?" she called, her voice rising with each name. She started to back out of the kitchen and backed right into her mother. She screamed a short throaty scream, and her mother jumped almost as high as she did.

"Esme! What has gotten into you?" said her mother, trying to keep the alarm from her voice. "And why in the world have you opened every cupboard in the kitchen?"

"It wasn't me, Mom. It was the ghost! I swear it. I came around the corner and she was looking into the cupboards and walking around inspecting the kitchen." The words poured from her mouth like water.

"Uh huh," said her mother. "And I suppose you're going to tell me that it was the ghost that left your dirty clothes on the bedroom floor."

"WHAT?" cried Esme. "I just put those in the hamper, Mom. I really did!"

"Sure you did, Es. Just like you didn't touch the cupboard doors, right, and they just opened by themselves. No, wait, by a ghost," her mother corrected herself. She smiled that all knowing smile she gets when she doesn't believe a word that's being said.

"Now I can honestly say I've heard everything."

Esme sighed. She looked at her mom, shrugged her shoulders in defeat and walked to the living room. She plopped down in a chair by the fireplace. From the corner of her eye, she saw movement in the chair across the room. She turned her head, and there sitting quietly, shushing her with her finger to her lips, was the ghost. Esme felt no fear, no fright. There was something about this girl that was fun and impish. She was just simply a little girl sitting quietly in a chair.

Walking into the room Esme's mom said, "Would you like to help me with dinner? I'm really sorry, Es, that I didn't believe you. I'm sure you saw something, it's just hard for me to believe in ghosts, you know?"

"It...it's okay, Mom," said Esme, looking nervously at the child in the chair across the room. "I understand. I've probably been thinking too much about what Vienne said."

Her mom crossed the room and sat down...on the ghost child. Esme shrieked and her mother jumped up, looking at the chair.

"What? What is it?" she cried.

As she jumped up, the ghost was still sitting in the chair holding her hand over her mouth, obviously stifling a laugh. Esme looked at the chair and back to her Mom.

"Oh, sorry, Mom...I...I...thought my laptop was in that chair. I guess I must have left it upstairs and thought I brought it down here." She smiled weakly. "Sorry, didn't mean to scare you."

Walking back into the kitchen her Mom said, "Well, come on in and you can set the table." Esme couldn't tell if she was mad, but she was sure glad she didn't get another lecture about ghosts.

"You're going to get me into trouble," Esme hissed. "What are you doing here anyway? Why can't my parents see you? Who are you?"

There was a pause, and the ghost child looked playfully into Esme's eyes.

She smiled again and said simply, *"You already know who I am."* Then with a small pop she abruptly disappeared.

Esme stood staring at the spot where the ghost had been.

*"This is too bazaar,"* she thought, confused and frustrated. *"First Butler comes to me on the beach and now this little girl, and she thinks I know her name. Yeah right. How could* that *be true?"*

Esme's head was spinning. She stared at the now empty chair struggling to put the pieces together.

There was a giggle from out of nowhere. Words formed in her head just like when Butler had talked to her on the beach.

*"Meet me in the attic tonight."*

## Chapter Eight

It was after eleven p.m. when Esme slipped out of bed and to the attic entrance in the hallway. She hadn't put on pajamas, but stayed in her signature jeans and t-shirt so she wouldn't have to get dressed after her parents were in bed.

Now, as she stood in the hallway staring up at the attic opening, where there was only one problem. The attic door was a good six feet above her in the hallway ceiling. She couldn't use a ladder because she didn't even know where to find one. She couldn't carry a kitchen chair all the way up the stairs because it would make too much noise, and she couldn't move one of the overstuffed chairs from a bedroom for the same reason. She wasn't even sure a chair would give her enough height anyway.

She stared at the attic door, trying to decide on a remedy for her situation. Suddenly she heard squeaking above her head. She looked up in time to see the attic door slowly open and the attached folding ladder start to unfold right on top of her. She squeaked and jumped out of the way. In the quiet of the hallway the noise from the ladder seemed deafening. She quickly looked around expecting her parents to come running from their bedroom to see what was going on. However, as the ladder came to a stop on the floor in front of her, there was no movement from her parents. She breathed a sigh of relief and looked up into the gaping, dark attic entry. There were no lights on up there, no way for her to see what she was getting into, which made her feel just a bit uneasy. Still, she knew the ghost child had to be up there, because she had invited her, hadn't she? And she was kind of funny, and a little bit mischievous, which made her fun in Esme's eyes. As she was about to put her foot on the first rung of the ladder a head peeked playfully over the side of the attic opening.

*"Are you going to stand there all night or are you coming up?"* Esme heard the words in her head.

*"Am I supposed to think words to you or do I talk with my mouth or what?"* She thought to herself.

*"Yeah, you think them, just like that. Just like you did with Butler,"* came the reply.

*"You know Butler?"* said Esme, stunned.

*"Of course I do! You know that. He's my best friend ever. Now, are you coming up here or what?"*

Esme hadn't really had her foot all the way on the rung of the ladder and as she heard the words in her head she started to lift herself onto the rung and her foot slipped off, causing her to bang her head on the upper rung.

"OUCH!" she said out loud.

*"Shhh!"* shushed the girl. *"You'll wake up*

*the whole house!"*

"*Oh, sorry. But that hurt!*"

"*Yeah, yeah. Get up here.*"

With no time to really even think about what she was doing Esme climbed the ladder. There was something comfortable about this little person, something familiar. She didn't feel afraid, she actually felt a little thrill of excitement.

"*Wait until Vienne and Delaney hear about THIS!*" she smiled to herself.

The ghost child grinned at her, happy to have a friend and confidante.

Esme grabbed the sides of the attic opening and started to pull herself up, but there was no need to pull. As she started pushing with her arms she felt herself lifted up through the doorway and set gently on the attic floor.

"*Cool! That was awesome! Can you do that again?*"

The ghost grinned sheepishly. "*Yeah, sure I can. But first you have to tell me my name.*"

"*What? Oh, I know what your name is. It's Rue. Don't know your last name though, just Rue. The Ouija Board said that was your name.*"

"*Not…exactly…true,*" She giggled treacherously. "*I was just messing with them that day. They only got it half right. And* you *know what the right name is.*"

*"What do you mean? How could I possibly know your name? I...I've never even met you before!"*

*"Oh yes you have. Just think, Esme. You were on a boat, a ship, a large ship..."*

Esme gasped, her skin prickling with goosebumps. Her voice came out in a hoarse whisper.

"How do you know that? How could you possibly know that?" she realized she wasn't thinking the words, but saying them out loud.

The ghost child's eyes sparkled as she smiled that knowing smile from the kitchen that day. *"I know a lot about you, Esme. I've known about you for a long time."*

*"But... how? I live clear across the country!"*

*"I...I'm not sure, really,"* she said thoughtfully. *"Sometimes I can see things, like mortals would see things on what they call their Television. Only, it's in my head, but I can see it. I saw you sleeping once. I saw you in a plane. I saw you standing and looking at the ocean."*

*"Well, okay, let's say all that's true. Why then? Why me? I'm nothing special, I'm just me. I can't think of a single thing that is special about me. Not really. I mean, I like homemade stew, but who doesn't?"*

The little girl gave a hearty belly laugh that

made Esme laugh, too.

Then looking thoughtfully at Esme she said, *"I guess I chose you. I searched thousands of mortals to find one able to understand me, to not be 'freaked out' as you are fond of saying. I wanted someone that would help me. Someone I could count on, and Esme, if there is one thing I know about you, I can count on you."*

Esme sat back, dumbfounded. *"How can you know that about me when I don't even know that about myself?"*

*"Easy,"* said the ghost, *"Because I see* in *you, not* at *you. I see your heart, what you think about other people, what you think about your family. I see how you beat yourself up because you don't take the time to see your heart."* She paused for a moment, looking at Esme like she could see right through her. *"You would love yourself if you could see what I see. At the very least, you would respect yourself for who you are."*

*"You know all this by just looking inside me."* Esme was skeptical. *"I'm just going to go with it for now, but I sure would like to see what you see. It would make my whole life a lot easier, that's for sure."*

*"You will. Just wait and see. So, then, what's my name? And hurry up, I wanna fly a little tonight. I never get a chance to have a flying buddy!"*

Esme thought back to the dream, or whatever it was, on the plane. It was still so vivid, so clear in her mind. She looked wide eyed at the ghost child.

*"LaRue,"* she said excitedly. *"Your name is LaRue!"*

LaRue clapped her hands and squealed with sheer happiness.

*"Do you have any idea how LONG it's been since I've heard anyone say my name? Well, except Butler, but do you? I mean, you have no idea how wonderful it is to hear that!"*

Esme was sitting with her legs folded beneath her and moved her leg to stand. Her leg just kept going into air, no floor, just air. She looked below her and giggled with surprise as she saw she was 'standing' a good foot off the floor. She looked up with excitement at LaRue, who was standing right in front of her, also in the air.

*"Come on,"* said LaRue. *"Let's fly!"*

The two girls spent hours flying through the attic, bouncing from the floor to the ceiling and then softly back to the floor. LaRue made a Ferris Wheel and shrieked with glee as they went around with lights flashing and real seats that rocked in a mild breeze. She made herself into a tiny ball of light and flew through the air over and under Esme as she sat in the Ferris Wheel. She showed Esme how she could see her when she was so far away. It was just like she said, like a TV set, only in her head. She could make Esme see the same things in her head, too. Each time she showed Esme something, the necklace she wore seemed to glow.

"*You got that from your grandmother, didn't you,*" said Esme pointing to the necklace.

"*Yes, just before she died. She gave it to me and told me---*"

"*It would save you,*" Esme softly filled in.

LaRue grinned. "*Yeah, that's exactly what she said! I KNEW you'd remember. I just don't know what she meant by it. After all these years, all it does is glow once in a while.*"

"*Can I see it?*" asked Esme.

"*I don't want to take it off, but you can look at it if you want to,*" LaRue said, holding it out for Esme to touch.

Esme held the small stone in her hand, careful not to pull on the chain. It felt cold to the touch and was about an inch long, cream colored, with four distinct sides. The top, where the chain connected to the stone was flat but the bottom came to a point.

"*Is it always so cold?*" asked Esme.

"*Not always,*" sighed the ghost. "*When it glows it gets really warm.*"

"*It sure is pretty,*" said Esme. "*I wonder why it glows.*"

Both girls shrugged at exactly the same time

and giggled.  Then, floating into the air they flew around the attic again.  Esme only had to think about being weightless and she would fly.  It was the most fun sensation she'd ever had.

Time went by so quickly, but soon Esme began to yawn.  Her eyes felt like sand boxes as she rubbed at them.

*"You better get some sleep, Esme, or your parents will wonder what you did all night,"* said LaRue with a grin.

*"Yeah, I guess so,"* she said, disappointed. *"But when can we meet again?"*

*"I'll catch up with you sometime,"* smiled LaRue.  *"I'll see you around for sure."*

The girls said their goodbye's and LaRue floated Esme through the attic opening and down to the hallway floor.

As Esme crawled in bed that night she heard LaRue in her head.

*"Thanks, Esme.  Thanks for being exactly who I thought you would be."*

As she floated off to sleep, Esme remembered LaRue saying something about helping her.  She wondered sleepily what she could possibly help her with, what she meant by that, and soon she was sleeping soundly, thinking of nothing at all.

## Chapter Nine

Breakfast the next morning was late. Everyone slept in and Esme's parents both were amazed at how long they had slept.

"How in the world could we have slept until ten?" said her mother in awe. "I don't think I've ever slept that late!"

"Well, I remember a few college parties going pretty late and getting some good 'sleep in' time the next morning, but not since then, for sure," said her dad with a smile. "What about you, beautiful? You seem to be a little groggy this morning. What made you sleep so late?"

Esme had a theory about that and it had a lot to do with a little girl named LaRue but she kept that to herself.

"Gosh, Dad," she said innocently. "I don't know, but it sure felt good."

They sat down together to eat a yummy breakfast of bacon, eggs, toast and hot chocolate. The kitchen smelled wonderful and Esme was starving. As she lifted her first bite to her mouth she looked across the table and there, with a place setting all her own, sat LaRue. She looked at Esme and smiled that "this is going to be fun" smile and picked up a piece of bacon, placing it neatly on her plate.

Esme stifled a grin and continued eating. She

looked from her mom to her dad, both of which were obviously not aware of the guest they had at the table. Deep in a conversation about where they would start with the weeding and mowing, they were clueless and Esme started to giggle. Her parents looked up expectantly.

"Oh, I was just remembering a dream I had last night," she said grinning. She glanced at LaRue and then down to her plate and started eating.

"What did you dream?" asked her dad, inviting her into the conversation.

"Oh, it was SO fun! I dreamt I was riding a giant Ferris Wheel and it had lights and music and everything! Then we flew back and forth around the attic and--"

Esme stopped abruptly as she realized what she'd said.

"Yeah?" said her dad. "You dreamed you were in the attic doing all this? That's funny! And who is 'we'? Who was with you?

LaRue started to giggle, but again it seemed only Esme could hear her.

"Oh, it was a friend in my dream. We spent the whole night—I mean dream-- flying and we could really fly! It was so fun!"

"I love dreams like that," said her mother with a smile. "They're the most fun to remember."

"So, Mom, Dad," Esme hesitated, as she

thought about how to ask the next question.

"Yes?" said her mother.

"Well, you know this house is on the ten most haunted houses in the country. So, do you think it's really haunted? I mean, have you seen anything interesting since we've been here?"

Her dad smiled his best adult smile.

"Well, Es, I don't really know if I buy into that whole ghost business. I mean, it seems kind of farfetched, don't you think?"

Esme glanced at LaRue and saw she'd made her head look like a 'Casper the Friendly Ghost' head and she was smiling broadly. She burst into laughter, and tried immediately to stifle it.

"Yeah, I suppose you're right," she said stuffing a bite of egg in her mouth to keep from laughing. "It's probably just a story to bring tourists here, right? I mean, who would want to spend the night in a haunted house, anyway?" she asked, as she vigorously chewed another bite of egg .

She looked at LaRue who had by now, shrunk her head down to the size of a grapefruit and was still grinning from ear to ear.

Esme laughed again and choked on her egg.

"What has gotten into you, Esme?" said her mother. "You're acting so silly!"

"I don't know," laughed Esme, swallowing, "I guess I just got the giggles or something."

LaRue continued sitting with the goofy smile on her face, which was now the size of a peanut and growing rapidly.

Esme started laughing harder and stood.

"I think I'm done, Mom," she gasped between fits of laughter. "May I be excused?"

"Esme, you sit down and eat. You've barely touched your breakfast!" said her mother, clearly frustrated by Esme's laughter.

LaRue immediately popped into space and disappeared. In her disappointment Esme stopped laughing and sat back down, regaining her composure.

"Sorry, Mom," she said quietly. "I think I'm ok now. I just got the giggles, I guess. Sorry. Yeah, I'll eat, I really am hungry."

They finished breakfast while visiting about what they would do that day. Esme occasionally stifled another giggle as she thought about the hilarious head LaRue was shrinking and blowing up. She managed to keep it to herself, but she decided she was definitely going to have to talk to that ghost about not getting her in trouble every time she popped in for a visit with the 'mortals'.

\*\*\*

After clearing away the dishes the family

gathered gardening tools from the storage shed and started working on the yard. Esme kept giggling at the memory of breakfast but was far enough out of her parents' earshot they, thankfully, didn't hear her.

She was working in the flower beds around the front of the house and her dad was mowing the back while her mother worked in the backyard flower beds. The sound of the lawnmower reminded her of home, and she thought again about Vienne and Delaney.

Her thoughts were interrupted when she couldn't find her trowel. She checked all around and stood up, thinking she was just not seeing it. But, truly, it was nowhere to be found.

She walked around the house to where she could see her mother working and stopped. Standing behind her with the trowel dangling loosely between two fingers and directly over her mother's head was LaRue. She was grinning that grin that always meant trouble for Esme. But Esme couldn't help laughing as she called to her mother.

"Mom!" she said laughing. "I, uh…" As soon as she spoke LaRue and the trowel disappeared. "Oh, never mind," she smiled. "I guess I forgot what I was going to say." With that she turned and raced to the other side of the house. She found LaRue spinning the trowel on the end of her finger and smiling.

*"I've got work to do! I have to get this done before we can hang out. Now, let me--"* She stopped and looked at the perfectly manicured flower bed, with not a weed in it.

*"How did you do that? And how am I going to explain how I did that? But cool! Let's go,"* she said with a giggle.

Esme walked casually around the house and called to her mother.

"I'm going to go explore the woods, Mom," she called. "I'm all done with the weeding."

Before her mother could question her, Esme was on the path to the woods and lighthouse. She glanced back and saw her mother walking around the end of the house to check her job. She smiled to herself. Having a ghost for a friend sure came in handy sometimes. Well, when she wasn't busy getting Esme in trouble, that is.

She walked into the cool of the forest, her feet crunching on dead pine needles as she walked. The air was clean with the scent of tree and brush. She loved how the Oregon Coast smelled! The trees were huge, standing as tall or taller than the lighthouse. They were magnificent. She found a dry spot of ground at the base of a large pine tree and sat down, leaning against the tree.

As she was thinking about the events of the night before, a face floated upside down in front of her. It was LaRue, and she was still smiling. Even though her whole body hung upside down, her dress stayed perfectly in place, just as if she were standing upright.

*"So, you wanna hang or what?"* she teased playfully.

*"Yeah,"* Esme laughed, *"But, that's not exactly what I meant when I said, 'hang'. Anyway, first, I have some questions for you."*

*"Ask away,"* said LaRue, turning herself to float gently to the ground feet first. She sat down in front of Esme.

Esme stared at the cute little girl sitting before her. Her blue eyes were the color of the sky, her blonde hair hung loosely about her face.

*"So, why are you here?"*

*"I was wondering when you would get around to asking me that. And the answer is, I don't know. I want to be with my family. Sometimes when my necklace glows I can almost hear them calling to me. I miss them. I really miss them. But I'm here, and they're wherever they are, and I don't have a clue how to get to them, or how to find them, even."*

Her face turned sad and serious as she spoke of her family. Everything about her changed, from the impish, playful kid Esme had seen so far, to a lonely little girl that just wanted to be with her mom and dad. Esme's determination softened when she saw the sadness in LaRue's eyes.

*"What can I do? You said you wanted my help, but how can I possibly help you?"* said Esme, feeling helpless.

*"I knew you would help me! I just knew you would! But that's just the problem. I don't know what to do. I don't know how to get back to my parents. I don't even know where they are, but they're sad, like me. We just want to be together."*

The two sat in silence for a moment until they heard a rustling in the brush beside them. From the undergrowth came the now familiar form of the oversized Great Dane.

*"Butler!"* squealed both girls in unison.

They ran to the dog and threw their arms around him. He wagged his tail and nuzzled both girls.

*"Well, hello to you, too!"* he teased. *"What have you girls been up to?"*

*"Oh, we were just talking,"* said LaRue, *"Wondering how I'm going to get back to my parents. You're coming, too, you know, Butler."*

*"Well,"* said Butler, *"That may not be possible, my friend. The most important thing is you are returned to your parents. Nothing else matters, not even me."*

## Chapter Ten

The small group sat together on the forest floor, just off the path leading to the lighthouse.

*"Oh, Butler, don't be silly,"* said LaRue. Then pointing her finger at him she said, *"You're coming with me and you know it."*

Butler nuzzled LaRue and said, *"I love you, too."*

Esme looked at the two of them and wondered what he knew that he wasn't saying.

She hugged the massive canine and said, *"Well, I think we've got some work to do. I need to understand better what happened after you, uh, well, after you…"*

*"Died?"* said LaRue, *"you can say it, you know. It's not a bad thing, for most people. And it's not a bad thing for me, it's just, well…not what it's 'spose to be, I guess. I've never been dead before, but I'm thinking I shouldn't be where I am."* LaRue grinned and instantly her head became the "Casper the Ghost" head from breakfast.

Esme burst out laughing. She held her sides, trying to breathe. LaRue looked at Butler and grinned that huge ear to ear grin that only made Esme laugh harder. Butler licked the bald Casper head and wagged his tail in amusement.

*"Okay, okay,"* said Esme, gasping for air.

*"We need to get serious. Stop doing that, LaRue! I have questions and I can't ask them if I'm laughing so hard I can't breathe."*

There was the familiar 'pop' and LaRue was back to her normal ghost self. She looked at Esme and smiled.

*"All right,"* she conceded, *"What do you want to know?"*

*"Well, for one thing, what happened after the ship section fell on you?"*

*"I don't really know,"* said LaRue, *"I think I died, and then I think I fainted, I think…"*

Her voice trailed off as she remembered the event that seemed so recent. *"I don't know, can you die and then faint? I mean, you're dead, right?"*

Esme giggled.

*"Ah,"* said Butler, *"but you're not actually dead are you? In the sense of the mortal world, I guess you would be, but among the immortal you are neither mortal nor immortal, yet. You are stuck in the middle. I guess WE are stuck in the middle, yes?"*

*"I guess I never thought about it before, but yeah,"* said LaRue, *"yeah, I guess we're stuck in the middle."*

*"Well, then,"* said Esme, bringing the group back to the task at hand. *"You say you fainted, when you woke up where were you?"*

*"I was underwater. There were people*

*everywhere. They were trying to get to the surface, but then they weren't there anymore."*

Esme looked at her in surprise. She looked at Butler. They both looked at Esme expectantly.

*"What? You both saw there were passengers in the water, and then there weren't any? They, what, disappeared…from the water? Could they have fallen below where you were, where you couldn't see them?"*

*"No, definitely not,"* said Butler, *"I could see clearly through the bubble and they were gone."*

*"Bubble? What bubble? Nobody said anything about a bubble!"* Esme exclaimed, looking from one to the other.

LaRue was staring hard at Butler, like there was a memory tickling the back of her brain.

*"A bubble? I remember looking around, I remember seeing people and then not seeing them, I remember…not feeling the water around me, and I remember breathing…air not water, like the first time I was in the water when Butler brought me to the surface."*

She continued to look into Butler's eyes.

*"That was a bubble? Where did it come from? How did we get inside a bubble?"*

Butler simply looked at her, not saying a word. He looked hopeful, encouraging, but remained quiet.

*'Sooo…"* said Esme hesitantly, *"What are you saying? You were inside a bubble? An air bubble? That seems a little out there, don't you think? I mean, you fall in the ocean and right into an air bubble, big enough to hold both of you. Really?"*

They fell silent, thinking about how or if something like that could even happen. They sat amid tall evergreen trees, birds chattered above them as the soft breeze tousled Esme's hair. She noticed LaRue's hair, oddly enough, lay softly, untouched by the breeze. The crashing of the waves on the shore beneath the bluff was muted, soothing the mood of the strange trio.

Esme continued with her questions.

*"Okay, let's just say it was…some kind of bubble. Tell me what happened after everyone disappeared."*

Butler began, *"The ocean seemed to boil and roll. We were tossed, and at one point sucked out of the ocean into the air then dropped into the ocean again. It was violent and LaRue was screaming, terrified. I did what I could to calm her, but couldn't get my footing to stay in one place. We were both tossed about quite severely."*

LaRue looked steadily at Butler, as though still trying to remember all he was saying.

*"How do you remember all this?* She asked, *"I remember it when you talk about it, but I forgot it*

*completely until you mentioned it."*

*"Fear does strange things to the mind, my young friend,"* comforted Butler, *"and sometimes the memory needs a little nudge to help it remember."*

*"Do you know how long you were in the ocean?"* asked Esme softly.

*"We had no way of knowing,"* said Butler, *"it was dark under the water and hard to tell the days from the nights. It felt like a very long time, though hunger and thirst didn't bother either of us. Probably due to our being caught in the middle, like we talked about. I feel it was probably several days, and we had no way of knowing where we were going. We were carried by the current, to the beach below, and eventually we were "dumped out" on the shore."*

*"Dumped out?"* asked Esme.

*"I remember that!"* exclaimed LaRue, *"it was like we were rolled out of a pan and onto the beach. That's why I didn't remember being inside a bubble. When we landed on the shore, the bubble was gone, we were wet from the tide as it pushed us further onto the sand. Then I only remember being here, on the cliff, in the house there."* She pointed to the Heceta House through the trees.

*"So, where did the bubble come from?"* asked Esme once again, *"And what was it? Who made it? How did they make it?"*

*"Butler, you remember more than me,"* said

LaRue looking at the Great Dane, *"where did the bubble come from?"*

The great animal stood up on all four legs and slowly stretched. He looked at LaRue with concern, as if wondering how he should say what he was about to say.

*"Where did it come from?"* he asked thoughtfully, staring into the trees. Then looking into LaRue's eyes he said, *"Why child, it came from you."*

*Chapter Eleven*

For two days Esme searched for LaRue. She was frustrated because she didn't understand why this revelation would have upset the girl so. She sat dejectedly on the porch step looking through the trees to the ocean beyond. Her dad stepped out onto the porch and sat down beside her.

"Why so gloomy, Es?" he asked.

"I dunno, Dad," she said, "It's just, sometimes I wonder what makes people do silly things."

"Like what?"

Esme looked at her dad. How could she tell him what had been happening the last few days?

"Well, before we left, Vienne was talking about her cousin. She said somebody told the cousin something that upset her and without even telling anyone, she just ran off and nobody could find her. Why would she do that? Why wouldn't she talk to someone and try to figure out the problem?"

"Ah," said her Dad. "That is actually a really common problem with people. And it could be a dozen things that would cause them to run. Some people just don't know how to express themselves verbally, so to try and talk something out is very frightening to them. Or, Vienne's cousin could have been told something that made her feel guilty, maybe she thought she'd done something wrong and was ashamed to face anyone. Kind of depends on what was said, I guess."

"OH DADDY!" exclaimed Esme, "You're absolutely BRILLIANT!"

Esme jumped up from the step and ran as fast as she could to her room. Her Dad sat on the porch, stunned.

"Did you hear that, world?" he said, looking around. "I'm absolutely brilliant!"

With that he stood up and sauntered proudly into the house.

\*\*\*

Esme shut her door quickly, grabbed some paper and a pencil from her carryon bag and sat down on her bed. Staring at the wall, she thought about what she wanted to say to LaRue. They were friends, she cared about the little girl, and wanted to help. What should she say to her?

*Dear LaRue:*

*I miss you very much. I am worried about you and we need to talk. Don't be afraid. Can we meet in my room tonight? Please don't go away, LaRue. You're my friend. I care about you.*

*Love,*

*Esme*

Esme wasn't exactly sure how she was going to get the note to LaRue. She needed to get into the attic somehow. But how? She folded her letter and stuffed it in her pocket. Jumping off her bed, she went to find her Dad.

She found him sitting in the living room by the fireplace, reading.

"Dad?," she asked in her sweetest voice.

"Yeah, Es," he said still reading his book.

"Dad, I want to go in the attic and see if it's anything like my dream. Can you open the attic door for me? I'll be very careful and I'll only stay there for a minute. I just want to see what it looks like."

He looked up from his reading.

"Well, honey, I don't know if that's a good idea. They may have stuff stored up there that they don't want people getting into."

"Oh, I won't get into anything, I just want to look. I'll come right back down. Promise."

"Well," he said setting down the book, "I don't see that looking would be a problem. Let's go see."

Esme bounded up the stairs, waiting patiently at the top for her Dad. They walked to the attic door and her dad pulled down the door, unfolding the stairs carefully.

"Looks like nobody's been up here in a

while," he said, wiping the dust off his hands. "Go ahead, have a look and then call me when you're done. I'll just be in the bedroom for a minute."

"Thanks, Dad," Esme smiled, "You're the best."

Her dad smiled at her and walked down the hall. When he was out of sight, she pulled the letter from her pocket and climbed the stairs. Poking her head through the attic opening, she looked around to see if LaRue was there. The attic was empty. She carefully unfolded her letter and lay it on the floor by the opening.

*"Please read it, LaRue,"* she said as she took one more look. *"I miss you SO much."*

Climbing back down the stairs she called for her Dad to come close the door.

"So, what did you think? What was up there?" he asked her, wiping his hands again.

"Nothing, really," she said wrinkling her nose. "It's just an empty old room, but pretty cool, really, for an attic."

Her dad walked back down the stairs and Esme returned to her room. She shut the door and sat down on her bed again. Would LaRue get the message? Would she even come? There was no way to know.

Her mom called her down to set the table for dinner. She smiled remembering LaRue sitting at the breakfast table changing her head size. She couldn't help hoping she would see her sitting across the table being silly. But LaRue wasn't there. Esme set the table and the family sat down to eat.

It was a pretty quiet dinner, but she managed to make reasonable conversation. Still, as soon as she could get her food down and excuse herself, she was upstairs in her room…waiting.

It was about ten pm. when her parents knocked softly on her door.

"Come in."

With worried faces they walked to her bed.

"Hey, Es," said her dad, sitting on the edge of the bed, "are you feeling ok?"

"Sure, Dad," she said, "why?"

"Well, you were just so quiet at dinner, and you've had a couple of rough days. Are you enjoying your time here in Oregon?"

"Yeah," she said, trying to sound excited, "I really love it here. It's just…well, maybe I'm missing my friends a little, but they're not even home. I'll see them when I get home. I'll be fine, really. I'm…fine."

"Ok, but you know you can talk to us, right? Anytime?" Her mom stood beside the bed, still looking worried. Esme thought she must not have been very convincing.

"Yeah, I know," she said, "and I will. I'm

fine, I really am."

Esme smiled broadly. They each gave her a hug and left the room, closing the door behind them.

*"Oh, LaRue, please come back. Please…"* she pleaded, looking around her room for any sign of the little girl. But there was nothing.

She picked up a book and tried to read, she put in her headphones and tried to listen to music, she wrote in her diary, she waited some more. It was almost eleven-thirty and her eyes were beginning to feel like sandpaper.

*"Where ARE you, LaRue? Aren't we friends? Friends tell each other everything. You can tell me whatever is bothering you. I won't tell anyone, it will just be between you and me. I promise, I PINKY swear."*

There was movement in the curtains to her left. She looked…and there standing beside the window, looking out, was LaRue. She seemed so sad, so small.

*"LARUE! You're back! Oh, I've missed you so much. Come, sit on my bed, let's talk."*

The child continued to stare, unmoving, out of the window. When she turned there were tears in her eyes.

*"It's coming,"* she said as the tears spilled down her cheeks. *"It has my parents, and it wants to take me, too. I didn't save them, Esme. I didn't. I*

*didn't know it was me, that I made the bubble that saved Butler and me. Why didn't I save my Mom and Dad, too?"*

The little girl sobbed uncontrollably. Esme walked to the window and knelt down in front of her.

*"What's coming, LaRue?"* she asked.

The little ghost didn't answer, but shrugged her shoulders nervously. She was still crying, and Esme felt her own eyes fill with tears.

*"How could you have known? You were such a little girl. You would have saved them if you'd known. You would have! Do you know how I know that?"*

LaRue turned and looked at her, waiting for the answer.

*"Because I see in you, not at you,"* she said smiling. *"A very smart ghost told me that once about myself. And now I see your heart, and it's a good heart. We're going to find a way to fix this. We are. We're going to work and work until we figure it out. I promise."*

LaRue wiped her eyes. *"But how? How are we going to do that?"*

*"I don't know yet,"* said Esme, *"but we're going to go over that ship sinking with a fine tooth comb. We're going to figure this out."*

The two girls walked to the bed and sat down. Esme was determined to solve this puzzle. They *would* figure out this puzzle.

As they talked and LaRue began, once again, to explain the ship and the sinking, Esme took notes. They worked until the wee hours of the morning, until Esme fell asleep while LaRue was talking.

But LaRue wasn't angry. For the first time since Butler had told her she made the bubble, she felt hope. They really *would* figure it out.

## Chapter Twelve

When Esme woke the next morning LaRue was gone, but she still had her notes. She barely took the time she needed to dress and eat breakfast, afterwards jogging up the path to the lighthouse and into the woods. They were going to need Butler's memories, as well, to figure this out.

*"Okay you guys, where are you?"* said Esme, settling down in front of the same tree as before. *"We gotta get to it."*

Instantly LaRue was sitting in front of her on the ground. Tears of the night before were replaced by the same wonderful smile Esme had grown to love. Esme smiled back.

*"Are you ready to work?"* she grinned.

*"Sure am,"* beamed LaRue.

Out of the same bush as before lumbered Butler.

*"Do you* live *in that bush or something?"* asked Esme.

*"Well, not like you would 'live' in a bush, but you could say I live there. It's really quite comfortable,"* said Butler as he walked to the two girls and sat on his haunches beside them.

*"Okay,"* said Esme, *"We know LaRue knows how to make the bubble. We know she made it big enough for the two of you. So, think LaRue, think*

*about how you did that."*

*"I don't know, I didn't even know I made it."*

*"Yeah, I know,"* answered Esme, *"But you did make it. What were you thinking about when the ship was coming at you?"*

*"Well…"* thought the little girl with a shiver, *"I guess I was worried about Butler. He was right there with me and I was afraid the ship would hurt him. I was afraid it would hurt me."*

*"Hmm…"* Esme was thinking about what she remembered of her dream. *"Okay, I want you to remember that fear. I want you to feel that fear again. Can you do that?"*

*"I…I…guess so,"* said LaRue. *"I can try."*

*"Okay,"* said Esme, *"Try to feel the same fear you felt that day, that moment."*

LaRue shut her eyes. Her face was sheer concentration as she struggled to remember the feelings of that awful day. After a few minutes she opened her eyes. Nothing happened.

*"Try it again, LaRue,"* encouraged Esme, *"but this time shut out everything around you and pretend you're actually in the water. Feel the water, feel the danger again. Try again."*

Butler walked over to LaRue and sat closer to her.

*"You must not push so hard, child. You must relax. You can do this. Don't be afraid of the fear*

*this time, you are in control, you can stop any time you need to. Just let it come and let yourself feel it."*

LaRue nodded to Butler and closed her eyes. This time she rested her hand on him as she concentrated.

Suddenly, everything began to happen at once. The necklace began to glow softly as LaRue and Butler floated into the air. The birds stopped singing and the scent of the forest was replaced with the smell of salty sea water. The area around them began to fill with what looked like water, but to Esme felt like nothing. LaRue's hair was floating as if carried by a current, as the necklace glowed brighter and brighter. Then, as suddenly as it happened, the necklace flickered and went out, and everything disappeared. Both ghosts were once again on the ground, birds were singing again and the air smelled of forest.

The three looked from one to the other, trying to think about what just happened.

*"The necklace!"* cried Esme. *"It's the necklace! It has to be. As soon as the necklace started glowing, everything started changing. It has to be the key."*

But LaRue was wracked with sobs, her face in her hands. Her shoulders shook as she tried to form the words to explain.

*"I can't…"* sobbed LaRue, *"I can't think about it, it's too…too…scary. I feel sick and I can't*

*find Mama and Papa. I'm afraid!"*

Butler stood up, tall and strong beside the ghost child. He nuzzled her neck and gently licked her cheek.

*"You must try again, my friend,"* he said, gently pressing his nose to her face. *"You must. It is the only way to save yourself and your parents. I will never let anything happen to you. Ever. Trust me, and trust yourself, LaRue. You were born to do this."*

Then, turning to Esme he said, *"You must remember as well, Esme. You must use your thoughts to be there with her. She needs your strength. We must all concentrate."*

Esme nodded her head solemnly and looked at LaRue. *"Can you try again? I'll be with you, too."*

Tears rolled down LaRue's cheeks as she closed her eyes. Esme focused all her thoughts on the dream she'd had, remembering the fear, remembering the terror of seeing the huge ship descending upon her. She stared at LaRue and Butler, centering her thoughts, concentrating on the two.

Once again the necklace began to glow, this time growing brighter and brighter. Her crying grew to great sobs as she remembered more and more. Around the three of them a thin wall began to form, sputtering at first, then growing larger and larger still. LaRue's sobbing stopped as she fixed her thoughts on the bubble. The bubble grew, enveloping the bushes and the trees, bigger and bigger it grew, expanding to… again the process stopped abruptly as, this time, the child collapsed on the forest floor.

*"You did it, LaRue! Did you see that? You did it!"* Esme squealed, jumping and clapping, hands in the air.

*"But at what cost?"* whispered Butler.

In her excitement Esme hadn't noticed the still form of LaRue, lying lifeless on the forest floor.

\*\*\*

Far out on the Pacific Ocean a disturbance boils and churns the sea and the air around it, unseen by man or machine. It is a strange tempest, one of anger, fury, and time out of place. The cries of hundreds of voices trapped within its bounds fill it, giving it form and substance as the beast races toward Devils Elbow. It has found what it once lost.

## Chapter Thirteen

"You have to do something!" yelled Esme as she fell to her knees beside LaRue. "Butler, you have to do something!" The words poured from her mouth, anguished and heartbroken.

LaRue stirred, lips moving slowly but emitting no sound

*"I'm… okay, I'm okay,"* She whispered. *"Wow, that was hard…it was amazing… but so hard."* She smiled reassuringly.

The words floated thankfully into Esme's head and she fell forward on her hands, dropping her head in relief.

*"You must rest now, LaRue, do not speak,"* said Butler, lying down beside her, the hackles on his neck rising. *"You must gather your strength, the beast approaches and our time is spent. It looks for you. You must have the strength to take back what it has stolen from you. But you must take back all it has stolen. That will require great strength, I fear."*

*"I don't understand,"* said Esme looking at Butler. *"She said something the other night about 'it' coming. What is 'it'? You call it a beast, what exactly is it?"*

Butler turned to Esme, *"I do not know what it is. I do not think it is of this earth, but it is evil and wants only to possess. That is how it survives. I have felt it many times, as well as those that are trapped within it, but only just now have I truly seen it's anger and darkness. I now understand how it has done what it's done to the mortals on the ship. None are dead, all are trapped inside the beast. It comes for this child, now. She must be strong enough to battle the evil, she must rest."*

Esme's head was spinning, she couldn't even imagine a beast or a 'thing' that could do this to people. How long had these people been trapped inside it? How long had LaRue and Butler been here? They had no concept of time, no idea of the passing of years.

*"I want to help,"* pleaded Esme. *"Please, tell me what to do, tell me how I can help her when she needs it. I have to help her. Didn't my memories give her strength just now? Can I help when the beast gets here? What can I do?*

Butler turned from staring out toward the sea. He rose and walked to Esme, looking intently at her for a moment before speaking.

*"This force is not to be trifled with. It will take you if you are not strong enough. If it senses you are fighting with her, it will seek you as well. If you are taken, your parents will never know what happened to you. You must think this through, young Esme."*

*"I don't care, I won't let it have her, I won't*

*let it have me. I will fight with her, I have to help her, she's my friend."*

Esme stared at the still form of the ghost child lying on the ground before her. She seemed so little to have this kind of weight, so much depending on her. She gazed at the strange necklace.

*"Butler, what is that necklace? How much more can it do? Will it work when she needs it to? How can we be sure the necklace will do it's part?"*

*"The necklace will work. It is very old, from the most ancient of earth times, but it does require memory to do its work. Your memories, mixed with hers, will give her the strength to fight the beast and release those it holds captive. You saw how it worked with all of us focusing our memories. We must remain focused and it will work."*

*"How much time do we have before it gets here?"* asked Esme.

Butler walked back to LaRue. He lay down beside her once again and layed his head in his paws, as if in thought. He lifted his head and turned to Esme.

*"Hours, possibly. It will be here soon, and I hope there is enough time for LaRue to regain her strength. When the storm rages, she must be on the beach, just where we were when we were washed onto the shore."*

*"How do you know this, Butler?"* she said,

eyeing him suspiciously. *"You seem to know an awful lot about this beast and the necklace. Why?"*

Butler looked at Esme and then LaRue, then laying his head down once again there was a 'pop' as both dog and girl vanished, leaving Esme alone in the forest with her thoughts.

*"What does he know that he's not telling?"* she thought nervously. *"I wonder if I'm going to get a chance to find out."*

As she walked from the woods, she again heard the same whisperings she'd heard with her parents the day they'd walked to the lighthouse. It was soft, unclear, and vague.

She stopped as she got to the edge of the forest and turned, looking for the source of the whisperings. There was a hope in the murmurs, something she felt she knew and she stared into the woods, now streaked with rays of sunlight.

*"I hear you,"* she said with conviction, *"I know who you are. We will save you, I promise."*

She stepped onto the asphalt path to the house hoping she hadn't made a promise she couldn't keep. Only time would tell.

She walked to the house and into the kitchen where her Mom and Dad were preparing lunch. They hadn't seen her come in, and she took the opportunity to really look at them. Oh, how she loved them. The possibility she may not see them again hit home. She walked quickly into the room and standing between the two of them placed an arm around each one.

"I love you SO much," she beamed, "you better never forget that."

"Well, now there's my beautiful daughter again!" laughed her dad, "and we love you, too. Now, make yourself useful," he said, handing her plates and glasses.

Esme looked from her dad to her mom. This had to work, it just had to.

## Chapter Fourteen

With lunch over and cleanup done, Esme was back in her room sitting crosslegged on her bed. She had been thinking about the ship, making herself remember the details so she could draw on them when it was needed. She was afraid, but if she was afraid then LaRue must be terrified.

From outside there was an earsplitting clap of thunder followed by a blinding flash of lightning. She jumped in surprise and looked to the window wide eyed. There, standing beside the curtain was LaRue. Esme stood and walked to the window.

*"LaRue!"* She exclaimed, *"You look so much better. Do you feel better?"*

LaRue smiled sadly at her and looked down.

*"We need to say goodbye now, Esme. Once we get to the beach I think it's going to get kind of weird."*

Esme hadn't even thought about not seeing LaRue again. She was stunned, unable to find the words to say.

*"I know,"* said LaRue, with the same sad smile. *"I feel the same way. I am going to miss you so. But how can I ever thank you for helping me, for coming here and being willing to do this for me. I'm going to protect you, Esme, don't worry. I won't let anything happen to you."*

*"I know you won't. After all, we're BFF's, right?"* Esme grinned.

*"Yeah,"* smiled LaRue, *"BFF's."*

Another clap of thunder rocked the house, followed by another brilliant flash of lightning.

*"It's time to go,"* said LaRue. *"I'll meet you on the porch."* She popped out of sight as Esme grabbed her hoodie and headed down the stairs. Taking two stairs at a time she called to her Mom.

"Hey Mom! I'm going to the beach, okay?" she said, hurriedly putting on her jacket. The last jump landed her in the entry. She ran to the kitchen as another rumble shook the house.

"Would you look at that gorgeous day," sighed her mother. "Have you ever seen such a blue sky?" she gazed contentedly out the window.

"Uh, yeah, right…Mom, in a hurry here. Can I go to the beach?"

"Oh, yes, that would be fine. But you stay out of the surf until we get there."

Her father's warning voice called to her from the living room.

"Es, we mean it, you stay out of the surf until we get down there. We won't be long."

"Yeah, I…I promise…no surf!" She yelled back as she ran for the front porch.

She came out the door and saw LaRue quivering, pressed against the side of the house, eyes wide, staring up at the sky. Esme looked up at the darkness that surrounded the house and beach. This was no ordinary storm. This was living, breathing terror and it pressed down on the earth around it with an evil that made Esme's skin prickle. She shivered against the icy cold that seemed to claw at her face and hands.

She turned to LaRue. The small ghost trembled and shook, unable to move from her spot on the porch. Esme remembered how she felt when she feared she would never see her mom and dad again. She loved them so much, and she never wanted to not have them in her life.

There was no way she was going to allow this little ghost to continue on without her family. Anger and indignation ignited inside her and she turned to LaRue. Opening up the front of her hoodie she spoke soothingly to the ghost child, trying to calm her fears.

"*Here LaRue, turn into that little round light you do and get inside. I'll carry you to the beach.*

She got no argument from the ghost as she quickly did her magic and flew into the protection offered. Esme zipped up and with one more glance at the churning sky, ran for the path as fast as she could. The noise was deafening and she couldn't believe her parents couldn't see it. How could that be?

There was little time to think of that now, and she forced herself to run faster, careful not to spill the precious contents of her jacket.

Out of nowhere came Butler, running beside her, down the path to the beach. His face a mask of concentration, the hackles on the back of his neck raised. Together they raced down the path and ran out onto the sandy beach.

The storm had reached such intensity that where there had been sandy beach there was now roaring surf. The water rolled almost to the picnic tables, usually far back from the waters reach. The thunder roared and lightning flashed continuously. Frenzied wind whipped at her clothing and blowing sand stung her legs and feet. The brush and trees bent and swayed almost to the breaking point.

Above her, the clouds fought for space, pushing and shoving against each other, boiling and rolling like an angry ocean in the sky.

*"Quickly, over here,"* called Butler, running to a spot on the beach. *"Everyone think about the ship. Think about the passengers. THINK! It is very important. Focus on LaRue and send her your thoughts."*

Esme quickly unzipped her hoodie and though the storm fought against her, the little ball of light scurried over the sand to the appointed spot, flickering dangerously. LaRue popped into her child form and huddled against her trusted friend, Butler.

Esme, Butler and LaRue concentrated on their

memories of the ship's passengers and crew. Gradually, the stone around LaRue's neck began to glow, brighter and brighter until her whole body glowed, as if part of the light.

But something was horribly wrong. Esme couldn't think, the fear of the storm overtook her thoughts and she wanted to run quickly to the path and back to the safety of the house. She looked around helplessly, her hands shaking and her legs feeling like they were buckling beneath her. A tingling sensation started at the top of her and moved slowly down her body. She felt stretched, her skin pulled and drawn as though she was being sucked through a straw. She looked toward LaRue and saw her misshapen face as it was sucked toward the beast. A deep throaty growl from Butler rumbled through their heads.

*"NOOOO!"* screamed Esme. Instantly Butler was at her side.

*"Do not look at LaRue. Focus! Think of your memories! Think, Esme, you must focus and think!"*

She could see Butler standing beside her and yet looking across the sand, there he was, standing beside LaRue, supporting both of them at once. She closed her eyes and focused on her dream, on the water, on the breaking of the ship, the screams of the people and the huge ship descending upon her. As she opened her eyes the bubble began to form, covering the entire beach. The storm continued to scream and growl, but now LaRue stood strong against it, all fear gone, replaced with that same determination Esme felt earlier on the porch. She was beautiful! Her face and body glowed and there was a peace about her now.

LaRue turned to Butler. The love she felt for him radiated from her face. Esme could feel her thoughts, could sense what she was thinking. LaRue now knew Butler must stay behind, and there was calm in the thought. The necklace shimmered as she removed it from around her neck and placed it gently around the neck of the dog. She stepped back and looked toward Esme, smiling as she gradually faded back into the small ball of light.

Butler stepped back through the wall of the bubble, nodding for Esme to do the same. The air outside continued to boil with angry screams as the beast fought to keep its prized possessions. Inside the bubble, the small ball of light she knew as LaRue, floated peacefully but alone.

Once outside, Esme pushed her way through the wind and blowing sand to where Butler was standing. There was someone standing beside him now. As she approached, she stared in wonder at the strange looking man. Butler nodded to her, there wasn't time to explain. The man was dark skinned and deeply wrinkled, wearing clothing of ancient

Native America. He was not affected by the beast and its rampaging, but stood strong and straight beside Butler. Staring upward, he slowly raised both arms to the sky, lips moving silently. Gradually, a small opening appeared in the top of the bubble. Small orbs of light, just like LaRue, poured through the hole – hundreds of them, weaving and soaring through the air within the bubble. His arms remained in the air until the last of the orbs was through.

The beast screamed a horrible deathly wail as the last orb flew through the hole. Its power gone, the beast fought to keep its form. What was left of the disturbance screamed again as a funnel formed from what remained of the storm, shooting hundreds of feet into the air. Now only a misty cloud, there came a hissing sound as the funnel shot up into the air and was gone.

The sand that had been whipping her legs dropped instantly to the ground, the waves, once wild and pushing against the shore, were sucked back out to the ocean, rolling gently back to shore. The sky was clear again and brilliantly blue.

The bubble disappeared and a bright shaft of light appeared above them. The orbs floated upward on the shaft of light to the soft sound of chimes in a gentle breeze and were gone, with it the stranger also.

*"LaRue!"* cried Esme as tears filled her eyes, *"LaRue!"*

She fell to her knees, tears rolling down her cheeks.

Butler padded over the now dry sand and lay down beside the sobbing girl.

*"Ah, sweet Esme, this is what you came here for. You did what you said you would do. She is with her family now, you must know this. They are all with their families, no longer prisoners."*

Esme looked at the dog as the realization of what had just transpired formed in her brain. She smiled through her tears as she stared at the warm sand. Seagulls called overhead, soaring through the air. She looked up and Butler was gone, but she could still feel him near.

*"Yeah,"* she sniffed, *"we did it, didn't we? We said we would do it, and we did it."*

Just then, her mother walked up behind her and touched her shoulder. Esme turned to her with a tear stained face.

"Oh, honey! What's the matter? I thought we were all through this homesickness."

Her Dad came behind her mother and looked in surprise at his daughter.

She gazed up at her parents, smiling through the tears, searching wildly for a reasonable explanation. She blurted out the only thing she could think of.

"It's so beautiful here. Doesn't it bring tears

to your eyes? I mean, just LOOK at it!"

Her parents stared at her, dumbfounded. Finally her dad spoke.

"I don't know this girl," he said, shrugging and shaking his head. Then running his hand through his hair and turning to the tourist packed beach he called out in a mock shout, "Has anyone seen my daughter?"

# EPILOGUE

Esme sat alone on the beach with her knees to her chest watching the water slowly roll in and lap lazily at her feet. Her parents sat a few feet back in their beach chairs, both with noses buried in books. She felt the gentle flow of the waves, filled with a sense of having accomplished something very special. She just couldn't wipe the silly grin off of her face.

*"This belongs to you now,"* said the now familiar gentle voice.

She looked to her right and saw Butler padding over to sit beside her. He looked down at the necklace now around her neck. Esme gasped and looked at Butler curiously.

*"Who* are *you?"* she asked.

*"I am the Keeper of the stone you now carry on that chain. The man you saw is my Watcher. He directs me, you could say. Through him, I am instructed to give it to the next mortal who will need it. That mortal is you, my friend, Esme."*

The stone lay cool against her skin. It reminded her of LaRue and she smiled as she touched it. She looked at Butler, confused as to why she would need something like this. She was just Esme, she liked homemade stew and rolls.

Butler chuckled, reading her thoughts. *"Well, 'Just Esme', you must trust me, for you will need that stone, just as LaRue needed it."*

*"You gave the necklace to her grandmother!"* exclaimed Esme.

*"In a manner of speaking, I guess. It would be more appropriate to say I 'delivered' the necklace to LaRue's grandmother. But that is a story for another time.*

*"But where will you go now?"* asked Esme, concerned for her friend.

*"I go where the stone goes, so I will go with you. With you I will stay until such time as you no longer need me, or until I am instructed to deliver the stone to another. Until that time, you have only to call me and I will come, as long as you wear the necklace I will hear you."*

Esme placed her arm around Butler's large shoulders. *"You talk funny,"* she giggled.

Butler rumbled with a soft chuckle.

*"BFFs."* Said Esme.

*"Excuse me?"* he asked.

*"You're going to have to trust me on that,"* she said, smiling back at him

\*\*\*

Note from the author:

I hope you enjoyed the first in the series "The Esme Chronicles".

Watch for the coming of Esme's next adventure,

# "Pirates of Shadowed Time"

Esme and her family travel to beautiful Dorningsworth, Maine for a genealogy vacation. To Esme, it couldn't sound more boring, but she soon learns there is more to this town than cemeteries and county records. Indeed, there are pirates afoot!

Esme is quickly wrapped up in the mystery of why they are here, what they need from her and how she can help them. Will she find a way to fix the damage they have done? Will she help them repair that damage before it is too late? With her best friend Butler at her side, Esme struggles to find answers to two hundred year old questions.

Made in the USA
San Bernardino, CA
25 September 2013